LADYBIRD
STORIES
FOR
4
YEAR OLDS

~ CONTENTS ~

The Gingerbread Man

Goldilocks and the Three Bears

The Three Little Pigs

The Gingerbread Man

Retold by Vera Southgate, M.A., B.COM
with illustrations by Daniel Howarth

*O*nce upon a time there was a little old woman and a little old man. They lived by themselves in a little old house.

They had no little boys and no little girls.

One day, the little old woman said to the little old man, "I shall make a man out of gingerbread."

"I shall make his eyes from two fat currants, and I shall make his nose and mouth from bits of lemon peel. I shall make his coat from sugar."

So the little old woman mixed the gingerbread. She cut out the man's head, his body, his arms and his legs. She patted them out flat on a baking tin.

Then the little old woman gave him two fat currants for his eyes. For his nose and mouth she gave him two bits of lemon peel.

She made his coat from sugar.

The little old woman put the gingerbread man into the oven to bake.

"Oh-ho!" she cried. "Now I shall have a little gingerbread man of my own."

Then she went about her work.

Soon the gingerbread man was ready.

As the little old woman went to the oven,
she heard a tiny voice crying, "Let me out!
Let me out!"

The little old woman ran to open the
oven door. As she did so, out popped
the gingerbread man!

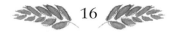

The little gingerbread man hopped and skipped across the kitchen floor.

He saw the door of the kitchen standing open and out he ran.

Down the street ran the gingerbread man. After him ran the little old woman and the little old man.

"Stop, stop, gingerbread man!" they cried.

But the gingerbread man only looked back and cried:

"Run, run,

as fast as you can.

You can't catch me . . .

I'm the gingerbread man!"

And they could not catch him.

The gingerbread man ran on and on.
Soon he met a cow.

"Stop, stop, gingerbread man!" said the cow.
"You look very good to eat."

But the gingerbread man only ran faster.

"I have run away from a little old woman and a little old man," called the gingerbread man. "I can run away from you, too." Then he cried:

"Run, run,

as fast as you can.

You can't catch me ...

I'm the gingerbread man!"

And the cow could not catch him.

The gingerbread man ran on and on.
Soon he met a horse.

"Stop, stop, gingerbread man!" said the
horse. "You look very good to eat."

But the gingerbread man only ran faster.

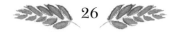

"I have run away from a little old woman, a little old man and a cow," called the gingerbread man. "I can run away from you, too." Then he cried:

"Run, run,

as fast as you can.

You can't catch me . . .

I'm the gingerbread man!"

And the horse could not catch him.

The gingerbread man ran on and on.
He began to feel very proud of his running.
"No one can catch me," he said.

Just then he met a sly old fox.

"Stop, stop, gingerbread man!" said the fox.
"I want to talk to you."

"Oh-ho! You can't catch me!" said the
gingerbread man and he began to run faster.

The fox began to run after the gingerbread man, who began to run faster still.

As he ran, the gingerbread man looked back and called, "I have run away from a little old woman, a little old man, a cow and a horse. I can run away from you, too." Then he cried:

"Run, run,

as fast as you can.

You can't catch me . . .

I'm the gingerbread man!"

"I don't want to catch you," said the sly old fox. "I just want to talk to you."

But the gingerbread man kept on running.

Soon the gingerbread man came to a river. He stopped at the riverbank and the fox came running up.

"Oh! What shall I do?" cried the gingerbread man. "I cannot cross the river."

"Jump on to my tail," said the sly old fox, "and I will take you across the river."

So the gingerbread man jumped on to the fox's tail.

The fox began to swim across the river.

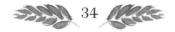

Soon the sly old fox turned his head and said, "Little gingerbread man, you are too heavy for my tail. You will get wet. Jump up on to my back."

So the gingerbread man jumped on to the fox's back.

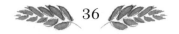

The sly old fox swam further out into the river.

Then he turned his head again and said, "Little gingerbread man, you are too heavy for my back. You will get wet. Jump on to my nose."

So the gingerbread man jumped on to the fox's nose.

Soon the fox reached the other side of the river. As soon as his feet touched the bank of the river, he tossed the gingerbread man into the air.

The fox opened his mouth and SNAP! went his teeth.

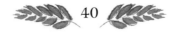

"Oh dear!" said the gingerbread man.
"I am one-quarter gone!"

Then he cried, "I am half gone!"

Then he cried, "I am three-quarters gone!"

After that, the gingerbread man said
nothing more at all.

A History of

The Gingerbread Man

The Gingerbread Man, also known as
The Gingerbread Boy, has appeared in films,
TV programmes, songs and novels.

The exact origins of the story of
The Gingerbread Man are unknown.
Norwegian writers Peter Christen Asbjørnsen
and Jørgen Moe wrote an early version which
appeared in the mid-1800s, called *The Pancake*.
A later adaptation, *The Fleeing Pancake*,
became one of the most popular versions
in Europe.

The Gingerbread Boy made his first appearance
in print in the May 1875 issue of *St. Nicholas*
magazine, but children were already familiar
with the story by that time.

The simple tale has inspired many
modern runaway food tales, including
Ying Chang Compestine's Chinese New
Year tale, *The Runaway Rice Cake*.

Goldilocks
and the
Three Bears

Retold by Vera Southgate, M.A., B.COM

with illustrations by Polona Lovšin

*O*nce *upon a time* there were three bears who lived in a little house in a wood.

Father Bear was a very big bear. Mother Bear was a medium-sized bear. Baby Bear was just a tiny, little bear.

One morning, Mother Bear cooked some porridge for breakfast. She put it into three bowls.

There was a very big bowl for Father Bear, a medium-sized bowl for Mother Bear and a tiny, little bowl for Baby Bear.

The porridge was rather hot so the three bears decided to go for a walk in the wood while it cooled.

At the edge of the wood, in another little house, there lived a little girl.

Her golden hair was so long that she could sit on it. She was called Goldilocks.

On that very same morning, before breakfast, Goldilocks also went for a walk in the wood.

Soon Goldilocks came to the little house where the three bears lived. The door was open and she peeped inside. When she saw that no one was there, she walked straight in.

Goldilocks saw the three bowls of porridge and the three spoons on the table. The porridge smelled good and Goldilocks was hungry because she had not had her breakfast.

Goldilocks picked up the very big spoon and tasted the porridge in the very big bowl. It was too hot!

Then she picked up the medium-sized spoon and tasted the porridge in the medium-sized bowl. It was too lumpy!

Then she picked up the tiny, little spoon and tasted the porridge in the tiny, little bowl. It was just right.

Soon she had eaten it all up!

Then Goldilocks saw three chairs: a very big chair, a medium-sized chair and a tiny, little chair.

She sat in the very big chair.

It was too high!

She sat in the medium-sized chair.

It was too hard!

Then she sat in the tiny, little chair.

It was just right.

But Goldilocks was rather too heavy
for the tiny chair. The seat began to crack
and then it broke into lots of little pieces.

Next, Goldilocks went into the bedroom. There she saw three beds: a very big bed, a medium-sized bed and a tiny, little bed.

She felt tired and thought she would like to sleep.

So Goldilocks climbed up on to the very big bed. It was too hard!

Then she climbed up on to the medium-sized bed. It was too soft!

Then Goldilocks lay down on the tiny, little bed. It was just right.

Soon she was fast asleep.

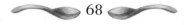

Before long, the three bears came home
for breakfast.

Father Bear looked at his very big porridge
bowl and said in a very loud voice,
"Who has been eating my porridge?"

Mother Bear looked at her medium-sized porridge bowl and said in a medium-sized voice, "Who has been eating my porridge?"

Baby Bear looked at his tiny, little porridge bowl and said in a tiny, little voice, "Who has been eating my porridge and has eaten it all up?"

Next, Father Bear looked at his very big chair. "Who has been sitting in my chair?" he asked in a very loud voice.

Then Mother Bear looked at her medium-sized chair. "Who has been sitting in my chair?" she asked in a medium-sized voice.

Then Baby Bear looked at his tiny, little chair. "Who has been sitting in my chair and has broken it?" he asked in a tiny, little voice.

Next, the three bears went into the bedroom.
Father Bear looked at his very big bed.
"Who has been lying on my bed?" he asked
in a very loud voice.

Mother Bear looked at her medium-sized
bed. "Who has been lying on my bed?"
she asked in a medium-sized voice.

Baby Bear looked at his tiny, little bed.

"Here she is!" he cried, making his tiny,
little voice as loud as he could. "Here is
the naughty girl who has eaten my porridge
and broken my chair! Here she is!"

At the sounds of their voices, Goldilocks woke up. When she saw the three bears, she jumped off the bed in fright.

She rushed down the stairs, through the cottage door and disappeared into the wood.

By the time the three bears reached the door, Goldilocks was out of sight. The three bears never saw her again.

Goldilocks and the Three Bears

Goldilocks and the Three Bears is one of the most enduring fairy tales and is well known to many children around the world.

In 1831, a woman called Eleanor Mure wrote a story about three bears for her nephew. A few years later, in 1837, a similar tale was published by the author and poet Robert Southey.

In both versions, it is an old woman, rather than a little girl, who enters the house of the three bears. It was only in a later version of the tale by Joseph Cundall, published in 1849, that the old woman was changed to a little girl.

The name Goldilocks appeared in the twentieth century. Until then, the little girl had a variety of names including Little Silver Hair, Golden Hair, Silver Hair, Goldenlocks and Little Golden-Hair.

There are several variations of the story's ending. In Vera Southgate's version, Goldilocks escapes into the wood and is never seen by the bears again.

The Three Little Pigs

Retold by Vera Southgate, M.A., B.COM

with illustrations by Sarah Preston

*O*nce upon a time there was a mother pig who had three little pigs.

The three little pigs grew so big that their mother said to them, "You are too big to live here any longer. You must go and build houses for yourselves. But take care that the wolf does not catch you."

The three little pigs set off. "We will take care that the wolf does not catch us," they said.

Soon they met a man who was carrying some straw.

"Please will you give me some straw?" asked the first little pig. "I want to build a house for myself."

"Yes," said the man, and he gave the first little pig some straw.

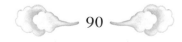

Then the first little pig built himself a house of straw. He was very pleased with his house. "Now the wolf won't catch me and eat me," he said.

"I shall build a stronger house than yours," said the second little pig.

"I shall build a stronger house than yours, too," said the third little pig.

The second little pig and the third little pig went on along the road. Soon they met a man who was carrying some sticks.

"Please will you give me some sticks?" asked the second little pig. "I want to build a house for myself."

"Yes," said the man, and he gave the second little pig some sticks.

The second little pig built himself a house of sticks. It was stronger than the house of straw.

The second little pig was very pleased with his house.

"Now the wolf won't catch me and eat me," he said.

"I shall build a stronger house than yours," said the third little pig.

The third little pig walked on along the road by himself. Soon he met a man who was carrying some bricks.

"Please will you give me some bricks?" asked the third little pig. "I want to build a house for myself."

"Yes," said the man, and he gave the third little pig some bricks.

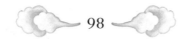

Then the third little pig built himself
a house of bricks.

It took him a long time to build it,
for it was a very strong house.

The third little pig was very pleased with
his house. He said, "Now the wolf won't
catch me and eat me."

The next day the wolf came along the road. He came to the house of straw which the first little pig had built.

When the first little pig saw the wolf coming, he ran inside his house and shut the door.

The wolf knocked on the door and said, "Little pig, little pig, let me come in."

"No, no," said the first little pig. "By the hair of my chinny chin chin, I will not let you come in."

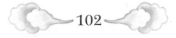

"Then I'll huff and I'll puff and I'll blow your house in," said the wolf.

So he huffed and he puffed and he huffed and he puffed, and the house of straw fell down.

The next day the wolf walked further along the road. He came to the house of sticks which the second little pig had built.

When the second little pig saw the wolf coming, he ran inside his house and shut the door.

The wolf knocked on the door and said, "Little pig, little pig, let me come in."

"No, no," said the second little pig. "By the hair of my chinny chin chin, I will not let you come in."

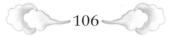

"Then I'll huff and I'll puff and I'll blow your house in," said the wolf.

So he huffed and he puffed and he huffed and he puffed, and the house of sticks fell down.

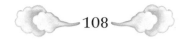

The next day the wolf walked further along the road. He came to the house of bricks which the third little pig had built.

When the third little pig saw the wolf coming, he ran inside his house and shut the door.

The wolf knocked on the door and said, "Little pig, little pig, let me come in."

"No, no," said the third little pig. "By the hair of my chinny chin chin, I will not let you come in."

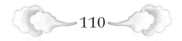

"Then I'll huff and I'll puff and I'll blow your house in," said the wolf.

So he huffed and he puffed and he huffed and he puffed. But the house of bricks did not fall down.

The wolf was very angry, but he pretended not to be. "Little pig," he said, "be ready at six o'clock in the morning and I will take you to Farmer Smith's field. We shall find some nice turnips for dinner."

"Very well," said the little pig. But he was a clever pig. He knew that the wolf just wanted to eat him.

So the next morning the third little pig set off for Farmer Smith's field before the wolf had arrived. He filled his basket with turnips and hurried home before the clock struck six.

At six o'clock the wolf knocked on the little pig's door. "Are you ready, little pig?" he said.

"Oh! I have already been to Farmer Smith's field," said the little pig. "I filled my basket with turnips and they are now cooking for my dinner."

The wolf was very angry, but he pretended not to be. Then the wolf said, "Be ready tomorrow morning and I will take you to Farmer Brown's apple tree. We will pick some red apples."

"Very well," said the third little pig.

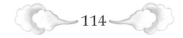

Next morning the little pig set off without the wolf again. He found the apple tree and was picking apples when the wolf came by.

The little pig was very frightened, but he pretended not to be. He said, "These are fine apples, Mr Wolf. I'll throw you one."

He threw down an apple, but it rolled away down the road. The wolf ran after it.

Then the little pig ran all the way home and shut his door quickly.

The wolf was very angry, but he still pretended not to be. He went to the little pig's house and knocked on the door. "Little pig," he said, "be ready this afternoon and I will take you to the fair."

"Very well," said the little pig.

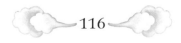

The little pig set off for the fair at lunchtime.
Then he saw the wolf coming up the hill
and was very frightened. He saw an empty
wooden barrel and jumped inside.

The barrel began to roll over and over down
the hill. It rolled faster and faster. It knocked
the wolf down.

The wolf was so frightened that he ran
away as quickly as he could.

The little pig jumped out of the barrel and
carried it home.

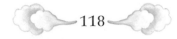

The next day the wolf came and knocked on the little pig's door.

He said, "Little pig, I did not go to the fair yesterday. A great big thing came rolling down the hill and knocked me over."

"Ha-ha!" said the little pig. "That was me, inside a wooden barrel!"

When the wolf heard this, he was very, very, very angry indeed.

He said, "Little pig, I am going to climb down your chimney to get you."

The wolf climbed on to the roof. Then he began to come down the chimney.

The little pig was very frightened, but he said nothing. He put a big pot of water on the fire to boil.

The little pig lifted the lid from the pot. The wolf fell into the pot, with a big SPLASH!

That was the end of the wolf, and the third little pig lived happily ever after.

A History of

The Three Little Pigs

The earliest printed version of this much-loved
tale was written by an English Shakespearian
scholar named James Orchard Halliwell,
and dates back to the 1840s.

The story in its best-known form appeared in
English Fairy Tales by Joseph Jacobs in 1890.
This story includes the familiar phrases:

"No, no, by the hair of my chinny chin chin."

*"Then I'll huff and I'll puff and I'll blow your
house in!"*

An animated film of the story was made
in 1933 and included the now-famous song
"Who's Afraid of the Big Bad Wolf?"

Cinderella

Based on the version by Vera Southgate, M.A., B.COM
with illustrations by Yunhee Park

*O*nce upon a time there was a young girl called Cinderella. After her mother had died, Cinderella lived only with her father and two stepsisters.

Cinderella's stepsisters were fair of face, but because they were bad-tempered and unkind, their faces grew to look ugly. They were jealous of Cinderella because she was a lovely child, and so they were often unkind to her. The stepsisters made Cinderella do all the work in the house. She worked from morning till night without stopping.

Cinderella not only did all the housework but she also helped her stepsisters to dress. She cleaned their shoes, brushed their hair, tied their ribbons and fastened their buckles.

The sisters had many fine clothes, but all Cinderella had was a threadbare dress and an old pair of shoes.

After she had worked until she was weary, Cinderella had no bed to go to. She had to sleep by the hearth in the cinders. That was why her stepsisters called her Cinderella, and that was why she always looked so dusty and dirty.

One day, the king decided to hold a grand ball for his son. There would be a great feast and people from all over the country were invited. Cinderella's stepsisters received an invitation to the ball, but sadly Cinderella was not invited as everyone thought she was her sisters' maid.

On the evening of the ball, Cinderella had to help her sisters to get dressed. She thought of how she would love to go to the ball and tears began to run down her face.

"I wish I could wear a beautiful dress and go to the ball," said Cinderella.

"A fine sight you would be at a ball!" The stepsisters laughed.

When they had left, poor Cinderella sat down and cried.

Suddenly, she heard a voice saying, "What is the matter, my dear?" There stood a fairy godmother, smiling kindly at her.

"I would like to go to the ball," said Cinderella.

"And so you shall, my dear," said her fairy godmother. "Dry your eyes and then do exactly as I tell you."

"First, go into the garden and bring me the biggest pumpkin you can find," said the fairy godmother.

"Very well," said Cinderella, and she ran off to the garden. She picked the biggest pumpkin she could find and took it to her fairy godmother. The fairy godmother touched the pumpkin with her magic wand. Suddenly, it turned into the most wonderful golden carriage one could imagine. The inside was lined with red velvet.

"Now run and fetch me the mousetrap from the pantry," said the fairy godmother.

There were six mice in the mousetrap.
Cinderella brought it to her fairy godmother.
With one touch of the magic wand, the mice
turned into six fine grey horses.

"Next," said Cinderella's fairy godmother,
"bring me three lizards." Cinderella ran
into the garden and there she found three
small lizards. Cinderella's fairy godmother
touched the lizards with her fairy wand.
They turned into three smartly dressed men.

There was now a golden coach, lined with
red velvet, drawn by six grey horses. There
was a coachman, in red uniform, to drive
the coach, and two fine footmen to open
the doors.

Cinderella glanced down at her tattered dress and her old shoes. "One more touch of my magic wand, my dear," said her fairy godmother. Then there happened the most wonderful magic of all.

Cinderella found herself in a beautiful ballgown of pale pink silk. On her feet were sparkling glass slippers. Cinderella's face was shining with joy. "Oh! Thank you!" she cried.

"Enjoy yourself at the ball, my dear," said her fairy godmother. "But remember, you must be home before the clock strikes midnight. For, on the last stroke of twelve, all will be as it was before and you will be transformed back into your ragged old clothes."

When Cinderella arrived at the palace, she looked so beautiful that her sisters did not recognise her. She looked so magnificent that everyone was speechless with astonishment.

The prince thought that he had never seen such a beautiful lady. He took her hand and danced with her all evening. He danced with no one but her.

Cinderella had never spent such a wonderful evening in her whole life. She was so happy that she forgot what her fairy godmother had told her.

Suddenly, the clock began to strike twelve. Cinderella rushed out of the door in such haste that she lost one of her slippers. The prince ran after her and picked the slipper up. It was small and dainty and made entirely of glass.

By the time Cinderella reached the place where her carriage had been, it had disappeared and she was in her old, grey dress. She had to run all the way home, as fast as she could.

The prince looked everywhere for her, but could not find her. He still did not know her name, but he had fallen in love with her and he was determined to marry her.

So, the next morning, the prince took the glass slipper to the king and said, "No one shall be my wife but she whose foot will fit this glass slipper."

The king's herald was sent through the streets of the city, carrying the small glass slipper on a blue cushion.

The prince himself followed, hoping to find the lady with whom he had danced. Every lady who had been to the ball was eager to try on the slipper. Each one hoped that the slipper would fit her and that she would marry the prince.

Many ladies tried to squeeze their feet into the slipper, but their feet were too large for such a dainty shoe.

At last, the herald, followed by the prince, came to Cinderella's house.

Each of the stepsisters was determined to squeeze her foot into the tiny slipper, so that she could marry the prince. But they both had large, ugly feet. Even though they struggled, neither one could force her foot into the slipper.

At last, the prince turned to Cinderella's father and asked, "Have you no other daughter?"

"I have one more," replied the father.

Then the stepsisters cried out, "She is much too dirty. She cannot show herself."

But the prince insisted and so Cinderella was sent for.

Cinderella seated herself on the stool, drew her foot out of her old, worn shoe, and put it into the slipper. It fitted like a glove! When Cinderella stood up and the prince looked at her face, he cried out, "This is my true bride!"

The stepsisters were horrified to discover that Cinderella was the beautiful lady who had been at the ball.

At that moment, Cinderella's fairy godmother appeared and turned her once more into the beautiful princess. Her old grey dress became a velvet gown. The prince lifted Cinderella on to his horse and they rode away together.

At the palace, the king arranged a magnificent wedding for the prince and Cinderella. All the kings and queens and princes and princesses in the land came to the wedding. The wedding feast lasted a whole week.

Cinderella never had to sweep floors or live with her stepsisters again. She spent her days in a beautiful castle, and Cinderella and the prince both lived happily ever after.

A History of
Cinderella

One of the most popular fairy tales, *Cinderella*
has inspired countless picture books, ballets,
musicals, operas, films, novels and songs.

The earliest recorded version, by Chinese author
and scholar Tuan Ch'eng-shih, was published
in the ninth century and entitled *Ye Xian*.
Today's popular retelling is based on
Charles Perrault's 1697 version called
Cendrillon, ou la Petite Pantoufle de Verre
(*Cinderella, or The Little Glass Slipper*).

The Brothers Grimm included the story
in their collection of tales published in 1812.

There are many variations of the story,
but the theme of an unlucky girl whose
fortunes change can be found in all of them.

Puss
in
Boots

Retold by Vera Southgate, M.A., B.COM
with illustrations by Daniel Howarth

Once upon a time there was a miller who had three sons. He was so poor that when he died he left nothing but his mill, his donkey and his cat.

The mill was left to his eldest son and the donkey went to his second son. Then all that was left for the youngest son was his father's cat.

"Alas!" The youngest son sighed. "Puss is no use to me and I am too poor to even feed him."

"Do not worry, dear master," said the cat. "Give me a pair of boots and a bag and you will find that we are not as poor as you think."

The miller's son was very surprised to hear a cat talk. "A cat that can talk is perhaps clever enough to do as he promises," he thought to himself.

 160

So, with his last few coins, the miller's son bought Puss a pair of boots and a bag.

Puss was delighted with the boots. He pulled them on and strutted up and down in front of his master. He looked so proud of himself that the miller's son could not help but laugh at him.

From that time onwards, the miller's son always called him Puss in Boots.

Puss slung the bag over his shoulder and went off to the garden. There he gathered some fresh lettuce leaves which he put in his bag.

Next, Puss in Boots set off across the fields. He stopped when he came to a rabbit hole. Then, leaving the mouth of his bag open, he lay quietly down nearby.

A plump rabbit soon peeped out of the hole. It smelled the fresh lettuce leaves and came nearer. They were too tempting. The rabbit's nose went into the bag first and then its head. Puss quickly pulled the strings and caught the rabbit.

With the rabbit in his bag, Puss in Boots marched off to the palace and asked to see the king.

When he was brought before the king, he made a low bow and said, "Your Majesty, please accept this rabbit as a gift from my master, the count."

The king was amused by this cat wearing boots and talking. "Tell your master," he said, "that I accept his gift and I am much obliged."

On another day, Puss again lay down
in a field. Once more his bag was open
beside him. This time he caught two
fine partridges.

Again, Puss in Boots took his catch to the
king. As before, the king accepted the gift
from the count. He was so pleased with
the partridges that he ordered the cat
to be taken to the royal kitchens and fed.

As it happened, the king had a daughter who was said to be the most beautiful princess in the world.

One day, Puss in Boots heard that the king and his daughter were going for a drive along by the river. Puss ran immediately to the miller's son and said, "My master, if you will do as I tell you, your future will be made."

"What would you have me do?" asked the miller's son.

"Come with me, my master," replied Puss and led him to the bank of the river.

"Firstly, you must bathe here in the river," said the cat. "Secondly, you must believe that you are not the son of a miller, but the count."

"I have never heard of the count," said the miller's son, "but I will do as you say."

While the miller's son was bathing in the river, the royal carriages came into sight. The king was in his carriage with his daughter and his nobles beside him. Suddenly, they were startled by a cry of "Help! Help! The count is drowning!"

The king, looking out of his carriage, could see no one but Puss in Boots, who was running up and down beside the river. However, the king told his nobles to run quickly to help the drowning man.

Puss ran back to the king as soon as the nobles had dragged his master from the river. Making a low bow, he said, "Your Majesty, what shall my poor master do, for a thief has stolen his clothes?"

But the truth was that Puss in Boots had hidden the clothes under a large stone.

"That is most unfortunate," said the king.
"We cannot leave him there without clothes."
So he gave orders to a servant to fetch
a suit from the palace.

When the miller's son was dressed in
a suit of good clothes, he looked a very
fine man indeed.

The king then invited him to go for a drive
with them. The miller's son sat in the
carriage beside the princess.

Puss ran on quickly, ahead of the carriage. He stopped when he reached a meadow where two mowers were cutting the grass.

Puss spoke to the mowers in a fierce voice. "The king is coming this way and he may ask you whose meadow this is. You must say that it belongs to the count."

The mowers were terrified to hear a cat talking in such a way.

A few minutes later, the king and his nobles
drove by. As the king passed the large,
lovely meadow, he stopped his carriage
and spoke to the mowers.

"Tell me," he asked, "who owns this fine
meadow?"

"It belongs to the count, Your Majesty,"
replied the mowers.

At that, the king turned to the miller's son.
"You do indeed own a fine meadow, my lord,"
he said.

Meanwhile, Puss had run further on along the road. He reached a cornfield in which reapers were busy cutting the corn.

"The king will soon drive by. He might ask whose cornfields these are and you must say that they belong to the count," demanded Puss.

The reapers, just like the mowers, were terrified to hear a cat talking in such a fierce voice.

180

A few minutes later, the king and all his nobles came into sight. Once more the king stopped his carriage.

"Tell me," he said to the reapers, "who owns these cornfields?"

"They belong to the count," replied the reapers.

"What a rich man he must be and how handsome he looks," said the king to himself. "I do believe he would make a good husband for my daughter."

Now, all the fields really belonged to an ogre who lived in a castle a little further along.

Puss in Boots hurried along the road until he reached the ogre's castle. Then he knocked on the door, which was opened by the ogre himself.

"Sir," said Puss, "I am on a journey and, as I have often heard how wonderful you are, I have decided to come and visit you."

The ogre was startled to hear a cat talking, but he was pleased to learn that the cat had heard how wonderful he was. He immediately invited Puss into the castle.

"I have heard that you can change yourself into any animal you choose," said Puss.

"That is true," replied the ogre, and he instantly changed himself into a lion. Puss got a terrible fright. He quickly scrambled to the top of a very high dresser, out of harm's way.

At once the ogre changed himself from a lion back to an ogre again, so Puss jumped back down.

"Sir, I must tell you that you frightened me," said Puss. "Yet it must not be too difficult for such a big fellow as yourself to change into a large animal like a lion."

"It would be even more wonderful if a huge ogre could change himself into a tiny animal," said Puss. "I suppose you could not, for instance, change yourself into a mouse?"

"Could not!" cried the ogre. "I can change myself into anything I choose. You shall see!" Immediately, he became a little grey mouse, which scampered across the floor in front of Puss in Boots.

With one jump, Puss pounced upon the mouse and gobbled it up. And that was the end of the ogre.

By this time the king's carriages were arriving at the castle. Puss in Boots, hearing the carriage wheels, ran to the gate. Bowing low, he said, "Welcome, Your Majesty, to the count's castle."

"My lord!" cried the king, as he turned to the miller's son. "Does this castle also belong to you? I have nothing so grand in my whole kingdom."

The miller's son did not speak but gave his hand to the princess to help her from the carriage.

They all entered the castle where they found a wonderful feast ready to be served. It had been prepared for guests whom the ogre had expected. Fortunately, the ogre's friends did not arrive, as news had reached them that the king was in the castle.

The king and the princess, the nobles and the miller's son all sat down to the feast. Puss in Boots stood by the side of his master.

The king became more and more charmed with the miller's son. When the feast was over, the king said to him, "There is no one in the world I would rather have as my son-in-law. I now make you a prince."

Then the prince said that there was no one in the world he would like so much for his wife as the princess.

And the princess said there was no one in the world she would like so much for a husband as the prince.

So the two were married and lived happily ever after, in the ogre's castle.

Puss in Boots was very happy living in the castle. He was always the greatest favourite with the king, the prince and the princess.

Puss never had to hunt for a meal again. He lived on the fat of the land until the end of his days.

A History of

Puss in Boots

The tale of *Puss in Boots* has inspired writers,
composers and many other artists over the
centuries. Recently Puss appeared as a character
in the hugely popular *Shrek* films.
Following Puss's success in *Shrek*, this lovable
feline went on to star in his own film,
Puss in Boots, in 2011.

The character of Puss in Boots we know
today is a male cat. But Puss was originally
female in early interpretations
of the story, such as in Giambattista Basile's
version included in his collection
The Pentamerone, published in 1634.

French author Charles Perrault
published *Puss in Boots* in his
Histoires ou Contes du Temps Passé in 1697
under the title *Le Maître Chat, ou le Chat Botté*.

The Magic Porridge Pot

Retold by Vera Southgate, M.A., B.COM
with illustrations by Marcin Piwowarski

*O*nce upon a time there was a little girl who lived with her mother, who was a widow. They were so poor that one day they found they had nothing left to eat.

The little girl went off into the woods to play.
She was so hungry that she began to cry.
An old woman came up to her.

"Why are you crying, my child?" she asked.

"Because I am so hungry," said the little girl.

"Then you shall be hungry no more," said
the old woman. She gave the little girl
a small cooking pot.

Then the old woman said, "When you are
hungry, just say to the pot, 'Cook, little pot,
cook!' It will cook some very good porridge
for you."

"When you want the pot to stop cooking," went on the old woman, "you must say, 'Stop, little pot, stop!'"

The little girl was so hungry that she wanted some porridge at once. So she said to the little pot, "Cook, little pot, cook!"

The little cooking pot did as it was told and began to cook some porridge. The little girl could hardly wait to try some.

When the porridge was cooked, the little girl said, "Stop, little pot, stop!" The porridge tasted very good and the little girl ate every little bit of it.

The little girl ran home with the cooking pot to her mother, and told her what the old woman had said.

"Now our worries are over," said her mother happily. "The little pot will keep us well fed!"

Whenever they were hungry, they said to the cooking pot, "Cook, little pot, cook!"

The porridge was always very good, and they always enjoyed it.

One day the little girl went out for a walk. While she was out, her mother felt hungry. So she said, "Cook, little pot, cook!"

The pot began to cook some porridge and the mother began to eat it. It was very good porridge and she enjoyed it.

She was so busy eating the porridge that she forgot to tell the pot to stop cooking.

The pot went on and on, cooking more and more porridge.

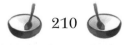

Soon the porridge began to come over the top of the little cooking pot. When the mother saw this, she knew that she must tell the pot to stop cooking. But she had forgotten the words!

The pot just went on and on, cooking more porridge. Soon there was porridge all over the table and all over the kitchen floor.

And still the little pot went on, cooking more and more porridge!

Soon all the house was full of porridge.

And still the little pot went on, cooking more and more porridge!

Soon, the house next door was full
of porridge.

And still the little pot went on, cooking
more and more porridge!

Soon all the houses in the street were full of porridge.

And still the little pot went on, cooking more and more porridge!

Soon nearly all the streets in the town were full of porridge.

And still the little pot went on, cooking more and more porridge!

All the people, from all the houses, came out into the streets.

No one knew how to stop the little pot from cooking more porridge. It just went on and on, cooking more and more porridge.

The people in the town began to think that soon the whole world would be filled with porridge.

Just as the porridge was reaching the last house in the town, the little girl came back from her walk.

At first, she could not tell what had happened to the town.

"Please stop the little pot from cooking any more porridge," cried her mother.

The little girl said, "Stop, little pot, stop!"

And then, at last, the little pot did stop cooking porridge.

Although the cooking finally stopped, anyone who visited that town from that day on had to eat their way through a lot of porridge!

A History of

The Magic Porridge Pot

The story of *The Magic Porridge Pot* as we know it today was recorded in *Children's and Household Tales* by the Brothers Grimm, in the nineteenth century. There are many similar tales in existence around the world, including a folktale from India about a pan that cooked endless amounts of rice when a single grain of rice was placed in it.

Ladybird's 1971 classic retelling of the story by Vera Southgate has contributed to the lasting popularity of the tale.